J 512.7 Mid
Midthun, Joseph
Numbers /

34028086196418
KT $5.00 ocn808810649
07/30/14

JOSE . 3 4028 08619 6418 HARRIS COUNTY PUBLIC LIBRARY :L HITI

W9-ATY-182

BUILDING BLOCKS OF MATHEMATICS

NUMBERS

WITHDRAWN
PRINT

WORLD BOOK

a Scott Fetzer company
Chicago

www.worldbook.com

World Book, Inc.
233 N. Michigan Avenue
Chicago, IL 60601
U.S.A.

For information about other World Book publications,
visit our website at www.worldbook.com
or call 1-800-WORLDBK (967-5325).
For information about sales to schools and libraries,
call 1-800-975-3250 (United States),
or 1-800-837-5365 (Canada).

©2013 World Book, Inc. All rights reserved. This volume may not be reproduced in whole or in part in any form without prior written permission from the publisher.

WORLD BOOK and the GLOBE DEVICE are registered trademarks or trademarks of World Book, Inc.

Library of Congress Cataloging-in-Publication Data

Numbers.

pages cm. -- (Building blocks of mathematics)
Summary: "A graphic nonfiction volume that introduces the history of numbers and number systems"-- Provided by publisher.
Includes index.
ISBN 978-0-7166-1436-4 -- ISBN 978-0-7166-1477-7 (pbk.)
1. Number concept--Comic books, strips, etc.--Juvenile literature. 2. Numbers, Natural--Comic books, strips, etc.--Juvenile literature. 3. Graphic novels. I. World Book, Inc.
QA141.15.N845 2013
512.7--dc23

2012031038

Building Blocks of Mathematics
ISBN: 978-0-7166-1431-9 (set, hc.)

Printed in the United States of America by
Worzalla, Stevens Point, WI
1st printing December 2012

Acknowledgments:
Created by Samuel Hiti and Joseph Midthun
Art by Samuel Hiti
Written by Joseph Midthun
Special thanks to Anita Wager, Hala Ghousseini, and Syril McNally.

STAFF

Executive Committee
President: Donald D. Keller
Vice President and Editor in Chief: Paul A. Kobasa
Vice President, Sales & Marketing: Sean Lockwood
Vice President, International: Richard Flower
Director, Human Resources: Bev Ecker

Editorial
Manager, Series and Trade: Cassie Mayer
Writer and Letterer: Joseph Midthun
Researcher: Lynn Durbin
Manager, Contracts & Compliance (Rights & Permissions): Loranne K. Shields

Manufacturing/Pre-Press
Director: Carma Fazio
Manufacturing Manager: Steven Hueppchen
Production/Technology Manager: Anne Fritzinger
Proofreader: Emilie Schrage

Graphics and Design
Senior Manager, Graphics and Design: Tom Evans
Coordinator, Design Development and Production: Brenda B. Tropinski
Book Design: Samuel Hiti

TABLE OF CONTENTS

What Are Numbers? 4

Early Counting Methods 6

Number Words 8

Early Counting Systems 12

Ancient Times 14

Roman Numerals 16

Counting Devices 18

Hindu-Arabic Numerals 22

Place Value 24

Showing Nothing 26

Working with Numbers 28

Glossary 30

Find Out More 31

Index 32

There is a glossary on page 30. Terms defined in the glossary are in type **that looks like this** on their first appearance.

WHAT ARE NUMBERS?
Hey there!
You've heard of numbers before, right?
Numbers are what we use to talk about amounts of things.
Numbers tell us "how many."
We can express numbers with words, gestures, or symbols.
Hey, it's number one...
...the symbol for one of something!
Howdy!
This number can show one of anything!
Like one shoe.
Or one apple.
Even one number!
We have some other friends, too!
HOP

We're the **base ten** system– 10 numbers that make up all other numbers!
You can use us to make any number you can think of!
Yeah, but where do we come from?

Good question!

Humans invented numbers a long time ago.

Raawwrrg!
Nope, I'm pretty sure it was humans.

We don't know *exactly* where or when numbers were invented, but we have some good clues...

EARLY COUNTING METHODS
We do know that people didn't always use written numbers.
They likely counted on their fingers when they were out and about.
To keep track of an amount, people etched tally marks on cave walls.
Or a piece of wood!
Or stones!
Or bones!
Each tally mark stood for one thing.
Much later, people invented names for different numbers.
Then they started to arrange the names in order by size.
That's counting!
0123456789

At some point, ancient Egyptians started to use different objects to represent groups of 10 things.
For instance, a single stone might stand for a herd of 10 sheep.
This idea made counting large numbers of things faster and easier!
Today, we continue to represent large numbers by using groups of 10.
That's why we call ourselves the base ten **number system**!
0 1 2 3 4 5 6 7 8 9

NUMBER WORDS
The numbers 1 through 10 have special names in most languages because people learned to count by using their bodies.
You can count up to 10 on your fingers and then start over.
Let's try!
0 1 2 3 4 5 6 7 8 9 10
One.
Two.
Three.
Four.
Five.
Six.
Seven.
Eight.
Nine.
Ten.
1 2 3 4 5 6 7 8 9 10
Give them a hand!

Okay, can we move on to the toes?
Um.
Let's not.
In English, the words used for the numbers after 10 are based on the first 10 numbers.
ELEVEN!
I'm named after an Old English word, *endleofan*, which means "one left over after ten."
And my name comes from a word that means "two left over!"
After ten!
So, what comes after you guys?
Drum roll, please...

Ta-da!
Thirteen!
Fourteen!
Fifteen!
Sixteen!
Seventeen!
Eighteen!
Nineteen!
0 13 14 15 16 17 18 19

It sounds like "teen," but it means ten!
10

I am 2 tens, but you can call me twenty!
20

I am 3 tens! Call me thirty!
30

I am 4 tens! I'm forty!
40

I am 10 tens! Call me one hundred!
I am 100 tens! Better known as one thousand!
See?
You can describe large numbers using groups of 10!
Keep 'em coming...
...I can do this all day long.
1000
100
40
30
20
10
0

EARLY COUNTING SYSTEMS
Eventually, people developed number systems, or ways of counting and naming numbers.
The ancient Egyptians used a system based on groups of 10.
Like you, they used symbols called numerals. Each numeral represented a certain amount.
The Egyptians had special symbols for their numbers, like these:
1
10
100
They also had symbols for big numbers like 1,000.
For 1,000, the Egyptians drew a picture of the lotus flower.
TINK
TINK
TINK
TINK
There are thousands of lotus flowers in the Nile River, even now!

Maybe the Egyptians thought a lotus was the perfect symbol for a big number like 1,000!

Egyptians wrote numerals from left to right, right to left, and sometimes even up and down.
To show more than one of anything...
...I repeat the symbol as many times as needed.

These symbols all mean 23.
crack

CRASH
Twenty-three!
Yikes!

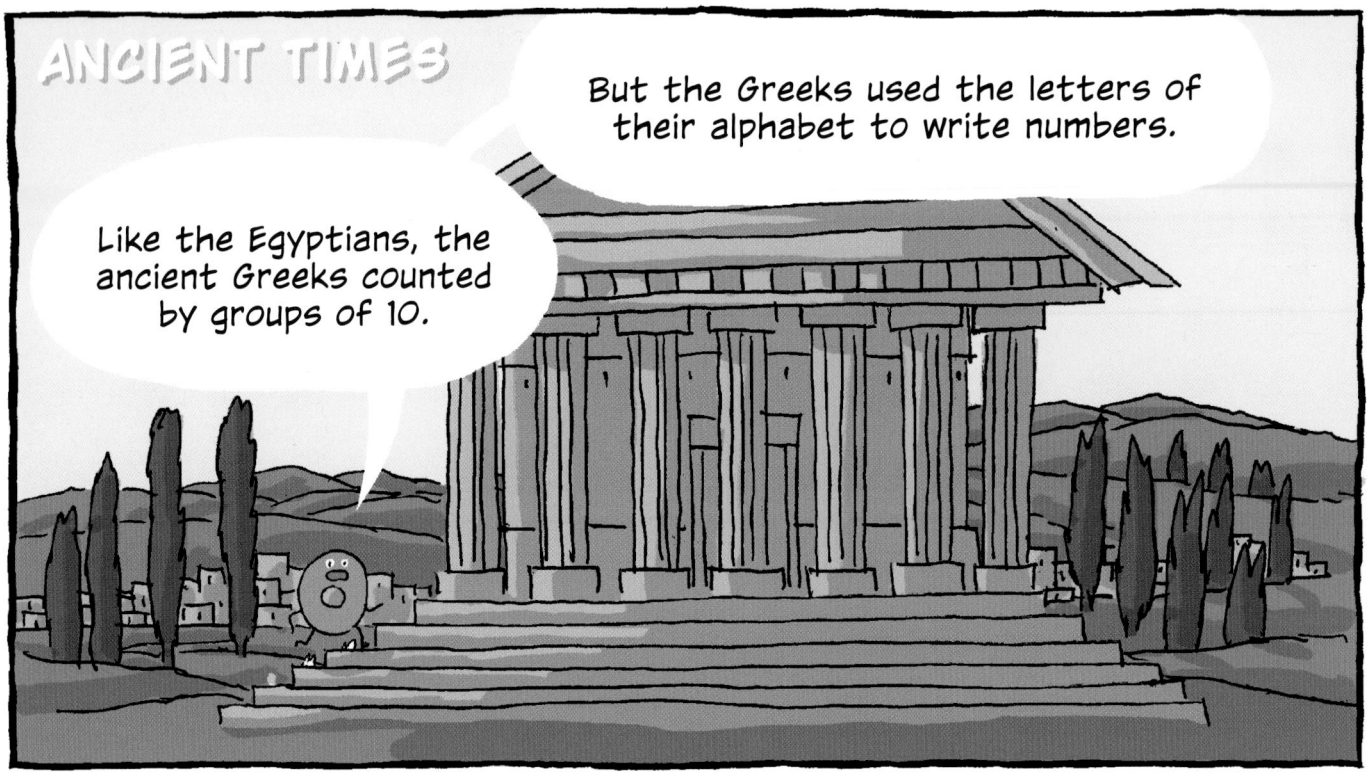
ANCIENT TIMES
But the Greeks used the letters of their alphabet to write numbers.
Like the Egyptians, the ancient Greeks counted by groups of 10.

The first nine letters stood for ones, from 1 through 9.
ΑΒΓΔΕϜΖΗΘΙ
1 2 3 4 5 6 7 8 9 10

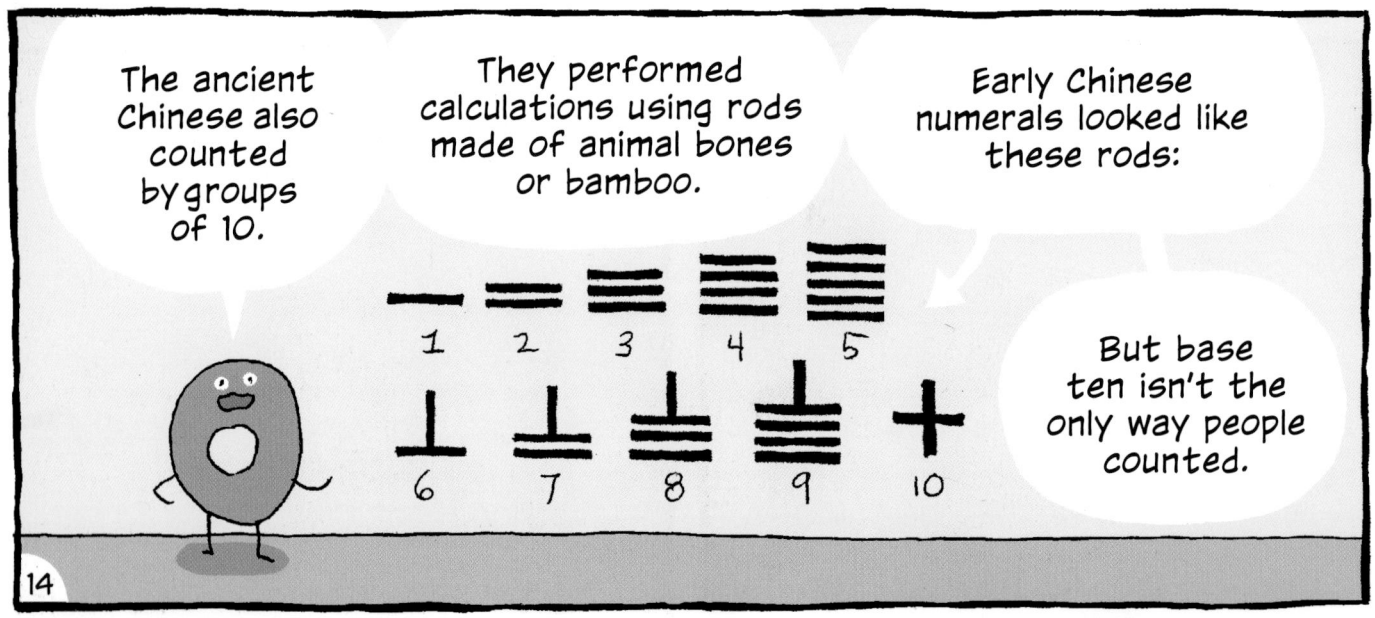
The ancient Chinese also counted by groups of 10.
They performed calculations using rods made of animal bones or bamboo.
Early Chinese numerals looked like these rods:
1 2 3 4 5
6 7 8 9 10
But base ten isn't the only way people counted.

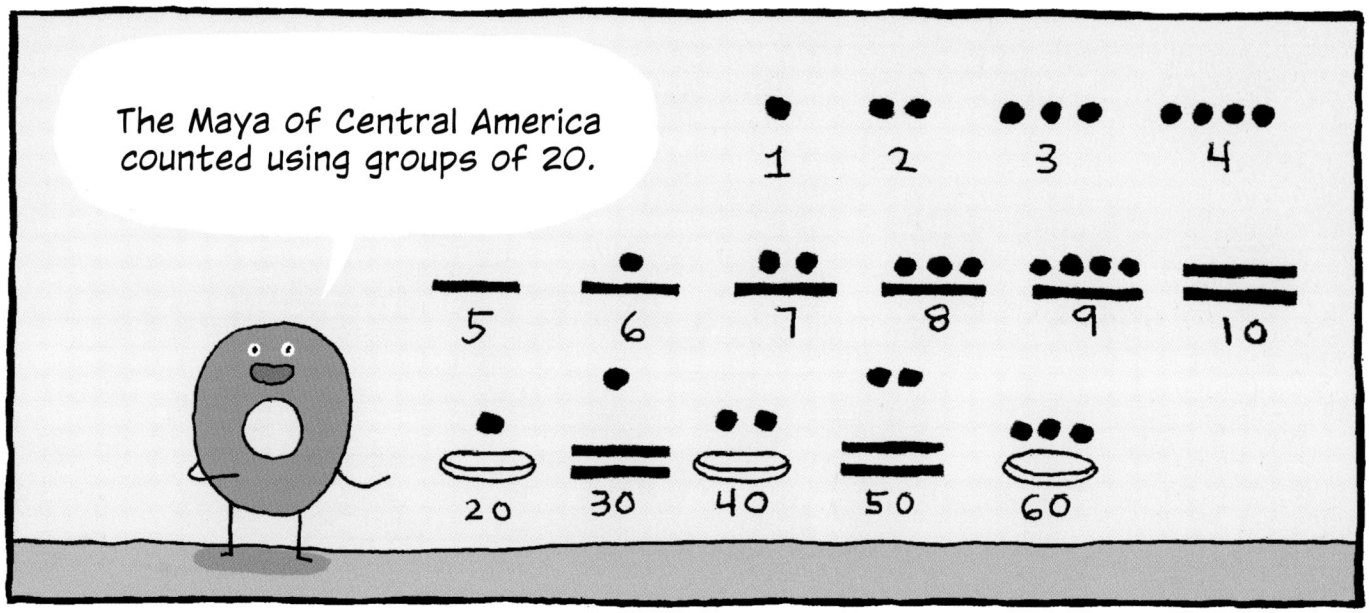
The Maya of Central America counted using groups of 20.
1
2
3
4
5
6
7
8
9
10
20
30
40
50
60

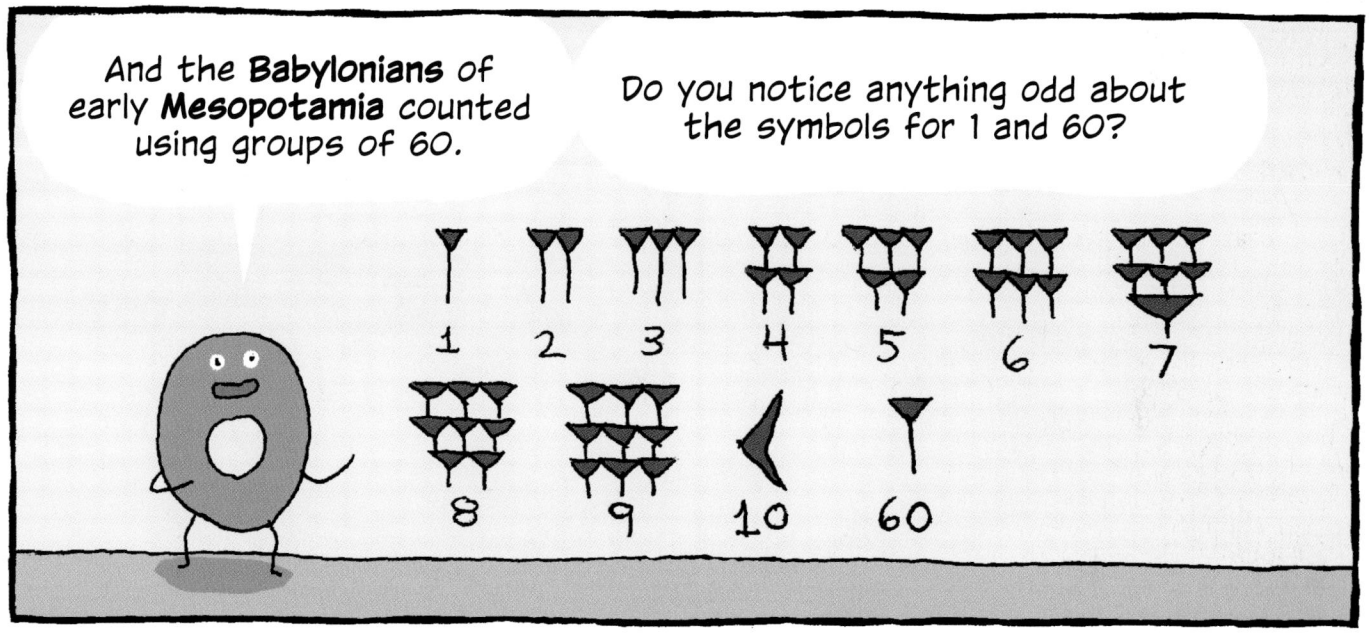
And the **Babylonians** of early **Mesopotamia** counted using groups of 60.
Do you notice anything odd about the symbols for 1 and 60?
1
2
3
4
5
6
7
8
9
10
60

They're exactly the same!
1!
60!

Imagine trying to solve a math problem using the Babylonian system!

ROMAN NUMERALS
Like the Greeks, the **Romans** used letters to represent numbers.
I II III IIII
1 2 3 4
V VI VII VIII
5 6 7 8
VIIII X
9 10

Did you know you can use your hands to make Roman numerals?

The numerals for 1, 2, 3, and 4 look like your fingers.
I II III IIII

The numeral for 5 looks like the space between your thumb and finger.
Try it!
V

And, the numeral for 10 looks like two crossed hands!

After a while, the Romans found a way to save time and space when writing out their numbers.
We used subtraction to make new symbols for the numbers 4 and 9.
The numeral IIII became IV and the numeral VIIII became IX...
These new symbols follow a rule:
The smaller numeral goes before the larger numeral to show that it is being subtracted.
The Romans also used other letters to stand for larger numbers...
L = 50
C = 100
D = 500

COUNTING DEVICES
People all over the world developed counting devices to help them work with large numbers.
One of the most popular early counting devices was the **abacus**.
Originally, the abacus was a tray or table covered with dust or sand.
Shake
Shake
You could make counting marks with one finger and erase them with a sweep of your hand.
Scritch
Later, people used tables marked with rows or grooves. People used pebbles or beads as counters.
The Romans even had a handheld device—a metal tray with grooves, beads, and a cover for travel.

A simple abacus can still be found in classrooms today.
Each column of beads represents a different group of numbers.
The column on the far right stands for ones.
The next column stands for tens.
The third column stands for hundreds.
The fourth column stands for thousands, and so on.
So when would you ever need to use an abacus?!

Imagine a distant galaxy in the far future...

On board your spaceship, you have 14 jars of Earth vegetables, *a rare delicacy...*

At a trading post, you decide to purchase 12 more. How many vegetables do you have now?
PSH

Normally, you would use your ship's computer to find the answer, but it's not cooperating.

And you're a little bit rusty at doing math in your head!
Why not use an abacus?

To show the 14 jars that you have, move up 4 beads in the ones column and 1 bead in the tens column.
Now, let's add the 12 jars you've decided to buy.
click click click click

Move up 2 more beads in the ones column...
...you've got: 4 + 2 = 6.
click click

And move up 1 more bead in the tens column. Now you have:
10 + 10 = 20.
Click

Add the 2 tens and the 6 ones together to find out how many vegetables you have in all.

Splrrb! Glp!
That's correct!
26!

That should be plenty of veggies to make a feast!

HINDU-ARABIC NUMERALS
Take a look at these symbols for the numbers 1 through 9...
Look familiar?

In ancient times, the **Hindu** people of India used these numerals.
Over many years, and with some changes, they have become the numerals that you use today!
A.D. 100-200's
1000's
1400's
TODAY
1 2 3 4 5 6 7 8 9

The Arabs learned about these numerals and began using them, too.
After the Arabs conquered most of Spain, they brought the numerals to Europe.
Because of that, the Hindu numerals became known as Arabic numerals.

At the time, people in Europe were using Roman numerals...
...and, they continued to do so for several hundred years.
But that was all about to change.
Across Europe, mathematicians began using Hindu-Arabic numerals instead of Roman numerals.
Hmm, I wonder why...
I+II+III

When you're writing out equations, it's easy to make mistakes.

And using Roman numerals for large numbers can make things confusing.
XXVII+LXIII
Squeak

With Arabic numerals, the same equation is easier to use.
27+63

That's because the Arabic numerals have **place value!**

PLACE VALUE
So, each *place* in a number has a different value!
An Arabic numeral can mean ones, tens, hundreds, or more, depending on its position in a number.
To better understand place value, let's take a look at some numbers.
In 25, the 5 represents 5 ones.
And I represent 2 groups of 10.
Together, we make 25!
In 50, the 0 stands for 0 ones.
The 5 stands for 5 tens.
Together, we make 50!

In 500, the 0's stand for 0 ones and 0 tens.
And, the 5 represents 5 hundreds.
500!
But Roman numerals, such as V, have the same meaning no matter their position in a number.
Five forever!
After European mathematicians made the Arabic numerals popular, other people in Europe started to use them, too.

SHOWING NOTHING
Wait–I almost forgot to introduce you to one of the most important concepts of mathematics–
Me!
I'm Zero!
You use me to show *no amount.* Zip, zed, nada!
Some number systems had ways to work around using a value for nothing.
The Romans and Egyptians had symbols for 10, 100, and more. But they had nothing for me...
Showing *nothing* as a *symbol* proved difficult–
But I can do it!
For example, to show the number 30, you can separate 3 beads in the tens column...
...and *none* in the ones column.
CLICK

The Maya were among the first people to use symbols for the idea of zero.
Later, the Hindus found a way to show nothing.
They created a numeral and called it sunya.
Sunya stood for an empty column on an abacus.
How enlightening!
By using just 9 numerals and sunya, the Hindus could write *any* number!
The Arabs used sunya along with the other Hindu numerals.
They renamed it sifr, the Arabic word for "empty."
The Europeans adopted the numeral sifr along with the rest of the Arabic numerals.
They renamed it...
ZERO!

WORKING WITH NUMBERS
You're saying we've all been around since ancient times?!
Correct! Although I am a little younger than the rest of you.
Even though numbers have been around a while, there are still new and exciting ways to use them.
Take the **binary number** system, for instance. It was invented *hundreds* of years after people began using Hindu-Arabic numerals!
The binary system is made of the numbers 1 and 0.

Today, we use it to program computers!
Hi!
Maybe you can find a new way to use an old number system...
...or, invent a new number system!
Once you know the building blocks of mathematics...
10, 9, 8, 7, 6, 5, 4, 3, 2, 1.
...the sky's the limit!

GLOSSARY

abacus a frame with rows of counters or beads used for adding and other tasks in arithmetic. The abacus was used by the ancient Greeks and Romans and in China and other Asian countries. Today, it is used in schools.

Babylonian having to do with Babylonia, an ancient region in what is now southern Iraq. Babylonia was the site of several kingdoms.

base ten a number system that uses 10 basic symbols: 1, 2, 3, 4, 5, 6, 7, 8, 9, and 0. The value of any of these symbols depends on the place it occupies in the number.

binary number a number written with only two digits: 1 and 0.

Hindu one of a group of people living in India.

number system a way of writing numbers. People in most parts of the world use the base ten number system.

place value the value of a digit as determined by its place in a number.

Mesopotamia an ancient region in the Middle East where the world's earliest cities were built.

Roman a citizen of ancient Rome.

FIND OUT MORE

BOOKS

Fun with Roman Numerals
by David A. Adler and Edward Miller
(Holiday House, 2008)

How Many Donkeys? An Arabic Counting Tale
by Margaret Read MacDonald, Nadia Jameel Taibah, and Carol Liddiment
(Albert Whitman, 2009)

Leaping Lizards
by Stuart J. Murphy and JoAnn Adinolfi
(HarperCollins, 2005)

More or Less: A Rain Forest Counting Book
by Rebecca Fjelland Davis
(Capstone Press, 2007)

On Beyond a Million: An Amazing Math Journey
by David M. Schwartz and Paul Meisel
(Random House, 1999)

One Is a Snail, Ten Is a Crab: A Counting by Feet Book
by April Pulley Sayre, Jeff Sayre, and Randy Cecil
(Candlewick Press, 2003)

The Story of Our Numbers: The History of Arabic Numbers
by Zelda King
(PowerKids Press, 2004)

Teeth, Tails and Tentacles: An Animal Counting Book
by Christopher Wormell
(Running Press Kids, 2004)

WEBSITES

1, 2, 3 Counting Games
pbskids.org/games/counting.html
Join your favorite PBS characters in learning about numbers and counting.

ABCya!
www.abcya.com
Choose your grade level to find number and counting games that are just right for you!

Count Us In
abc.net.au/countusin
The games and activities at this site are perfect for practicing number skills.

Gamequarium: Place Value Games
www.gamequarium.com/placevalue.html
This teacher-designed website provides many pages of games for practice with place value and other number skills.

Roman Numerals Games
www.roman-numerals.org/games.html
Learn about Roman numerals here and test your knowledge as you go!

Tamba's Abacus
www.bbc.co.uk/cbeebies/tikkabilla/games/tikkabilla-tambasabacus
Sing and count along with a colorful online abacus at this site from the BBC.

Harris County Public Library
Houston, Texas

abacus, 18-21, 26-27
alphabet, 14, 16-17
Arabic numerals.
  See Hindu-Arabic numerals
Arabs, ancient, 22, 27

Babylonians, 15
base ten system, 5
  beginning of, 7
  in Arabic numerals, 24-25
  number names in, 8-11
  of Chinese, 14
  of Egyptians, 7, 12-13
  of Greeks, 14
  on abacus, 19
binary number system, 28-29

Chinese, ancient, 14
counting
  early methods of, 6-7, 12-13
  on abacus, 18-21
  on fingers, 8-9
  See also numbers

Egyptians, ancient, 7, 12-13, 26

Greeks, ancient, 14

Hindu-Arabic numerals, 22-23, 28
  place value in, 24-25
  zero in, 27

India, 22

lotus symbol, 12-13

Maya, 15, 27

numbers, 4-5
  Babylonian, 15
  Chinese, 14
  Egyptian, 6-7, 12-13
  Greek, 14
  Hindu-Arabic, 22-23
  invention of, 5
  Mayan, 15
  Roman, 16-17
  words for, 8-11

See also base ten system; counting

place value, 23-25

Roman numerals, 16-17, 25
  addition with, 23
  zero in, 26
Romans, 16-17
  abacus of, 18

sifr, 27
sunya, 27

tally marks, 6

zero
  and place value, 24-25
  invention of, 26-27